Roobarb

The Birds

GO TEAM

Poodle
Princess

Roobarb
& Custard™

Meet the gang!

Mole

Custard

Mouse

Moggy
Malone

When there was a ballet

www.roobarbandcustard.tv © 1974-2009 A&B TV limited. All rights reserved. Roobarb & Custard created by Grange Calveley.

© Mogzilla 2010 www.mogzilla.co.uk/roobarbandcustard ISBN: 978-1-906132-2-00 Printed in Malta. 5 4 3 2 1

It was a bitterly cold afternoon. Roobarb and Custard shivered in the wind and snow as they trecked across the garden.

Moggy and Princess had been holding an evening singing session, but their voices were whisked away by the wind.

'It's not fit for a dog to be out,' Custard grumbled.
'Nonsense!' said Roobarb. 'This chilly weather means tomorrow's conditions should be perfect for my spectacular ballet-on-ice!'

'Eh?' said a frosty Custard.

'I'm planning a special performance of Duckpond on Ice,'
declared Roobarb, 'and rehearsals have already begun!'
With that, he twirled off.

First thing next morning, Roobarb raised his weather-forecast gear into the sky.

Results: H20=freezing.

Everyone helped to prepare for the show.

Post Dog's dogsbodies set out chairs,

while the birds practiced their acrobatics.

Meanwhile, Moggy ran through her scales, and Poodle Princess howled 'red lorry, yellow lorry, red lorry, yellow lorry.'

At 7 o'clock, the lights were lit and the crowds arrived. Everything was ready.

'I announce this ballet-on-ice... open!' trilled Poodle Princess. But her voice was drowned out by Moggy's opening aria.

Custard, as Dame Mange Blancmange, gave a thumping pas du chat onto the ice. Rover, as the Prince, skated over, bowing low.

With a skillful pirouette, he span Custard far too fast.

But Custard had stage-fright, and stood frozen to the spot.

Suddenly, out of the wings, the birds pushed their way to the front of the stage.

They began to show off their

stupefying balancing act,

perilous plate-spinning

and death-defying sumersaults... on ice!

The audience loved it. They applauded loudly as the birds jumped and span. Everyone agreed that this was proper entertainment.

Rover skated on, but there was nothing he could do - Custard had frozen, and the birds had stolen the show.

As the birds took bow after bow, Custard and Rover slid off-stage in a dramatic huff.

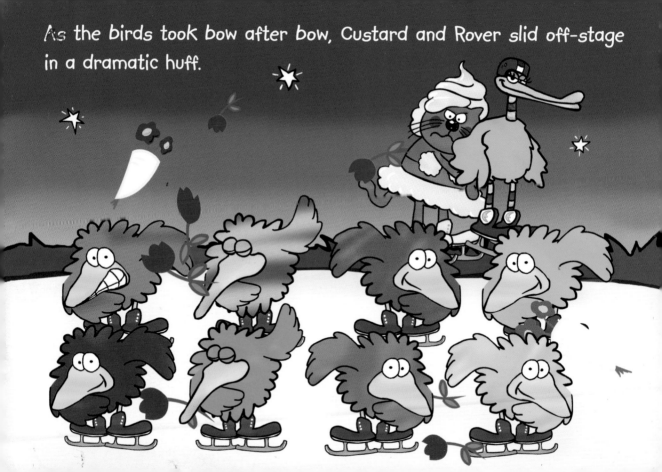

As Roobarb went up to take his bow, the ice gave in.

Poodle Princess finally got a word in:

'The end!'

Bag yourself more Roobarb & Custard books online at

www.mogzilla.co.uk/shop

'The gentle wit and charm of these new Roobarb stories will delight toddlers and parents. Young children will love the chaos that ensues not just between the forever joking Roobarb, the green dog and the wacky pink cat, Custard but with the rest of their gang too...it's guaranteed to be laugh-out-loud funny. Great for parents to read aloud with their children.'

'...faithfully crammed with all the slapstick and layers of subtler humour you'd expect. Simultaneously nostalgic and fresh, they're bound to please those who remember this green and pink pair from the first time around, as well as a new generation of fans.'

Teach Primary Magazine

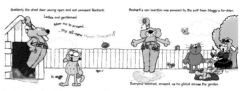

When Roobarb's trousers flew
ISBN: 978-1-906132-14-9 (large format)

When Roobarb found the hieroglyphics
ISBN: 978-1-906132-11-8 (large format)

When Custard was grounded
ISBN: 978-1-906132-10-1 (large format)

When there was a pottery party
ISBN: 978-1-906132-12-5 (large format)

When there was a ballet
ISBN: 978-1-906132-13-2 (large format)

Roobarb & Custard in your pocket!

When Roobarb found the hieroglyphics
ISBN: 978-1-906132-18-7
Pocket size

When there was a pottery party
ISBN: 978-1-906132-1-94
Pocket size

When Custard was grounded
ISBN: 978-1-906132-17-0
Pocket size

You can order any of these fab little titles from www.mogzilla.co.uk